MW00892344

XS

To Pattie Castor, Sue Hubacher,
and Holly Allan; three of the
wisest women I know—DDM

In memory of my agent,
Tema Siegel—DM

Published in 2006 by Concordia Publishing House
3558 S. Jefferson Avenue, St. Louis, MO 63118-3968
1-800-325-3040 • www.cph.org

Text copyright © 2006 by Dandi Daley Mackall
Illustrations copyright © 2006 Concordia Publishing House

Manufactured in China

1 2 3 4 5 6 7 8 9 10   15 14 13 12 11 10 09 08 07 06

THREE WISE WOMEN OF CHRISTMAS

Written by Dandi Daley Mackall
Illustrated by Diana Magnuson

CONCORDIA PUBLISHING HOUSE · SAINT LOUIS

Before the Wise Men from the East mounted camels to follow a bright star . . .
Before the Wise Men loaded gifts of gold, frankincense,
and myrrh for the newborn king . . .

There were three wise women:
Elizabeth, Mary, & Anna.

Elizabeth's Story

I was too old to have a baby. Everybody said so. But God was about to surprise us all with His gift.

My husband, Zechariah, had been away, serving as priest in God's holy temple.

I would not feel this lonely, I thought, as I gazed out toward Jerusalem, *if I had a child.*

Suddenly, Zechariah appeared over the crest of the hill. He was running like a man half his age.

I hurried to meet him. "What is it Zechariah?"

My heart quickened. He had been given a message from the angel Gabriel that he'd failed to believe, and now he could not speak.

I watched my husband's hands fly in the air like frightened birds. "I don't understand!" I cried.

Then Zechariah pointed to heaven and touched my belly. And I knew.

"God is giving us a child!" I exclaimed. And I hugged my belly and laughed.

The first wise woman received her gift. In her wisdom, Elizabeth raised the child, who came to be known as John the Baptist. He prepared the world for an even greater Gift, a Gift that would come through the second wise woman.

Mary's Story

"How can this be?"

That's what I asked when the angel Gabriel announced that God was sending me the greatest Gift anyone could ever receive.

I was alone when the angel burst into my presence
with the light of a thousand stars.

"Don't be afraid, Mary! God has chosen you. You
will have a baby and name Him Jesus, and He *is*
the Son of the Most High God!"

I was young and poor, a virgin engaged to Joseph
the carpenter. "How can this be?" I asked.

"Nothing will be impossible with God," the angel
reminded me. Then he told me of another gift:
"For even Elizabeth is to have a child in her old age."

I took courage from God's promise to my aunt.
"I am your servant," I replied. "Let it be done to
me as you have said."

And it was all done just as the angel said. In a stable in Bethlehem, Jesus was born, God's holy Gift. And this gift was the Savior, the hope of the whole world.

Young Mary was wise beyond her years.
When the time came for Mary and Joseph to
dedicate Jesus according to Jewish law, they took
their gift to the Temple of Jerusalem. And there,
waiting for the Messiah, was the third wise woman.

Anna's Story

They said I should give up. I was such an old woman, a widow of eighty-four years, never leaving the temple. Hadn't I waited long enough to see God's gift of the Messiah?

My back bent like the willows of Babylon,
I went about my daily temple duties, fasting
and praying. "God is sending us a Savior!"
I prophesied to all who would listen.

Then one day, something was different.
I heard the bleating of sacrificial lambs, as on
every day, the clang of coins in the offering.
But on this day, as my weak eyes searched
the sea of worshipers, the crowd seemed to fade,
leaving only one tiny baby before me.

I knew at once, this was God's gift, the Messiah.

I held the child I had been waiting my whole life to see. Then I turned to the people. "He's here!" I announced. "God has sent us His Son!"

A lifetime of waiting on God had made Anna wise. When the promised gift arrived, the third wise woman embraced the Savior and introduced Him to others.

Elizabeth held her son, John, and pointed to
the bright star in the sky. "Soon," she whispered,
"you will prepare the world for God's great gift, Jesus."

Anna sat on the steps of the temple and gazed at the
Jerusalem sky, grateful that God had let her live to see
His great gift—the Messiah.

Under the brightest star in the sky, Mary rocked her son, Jesus, and pondered the words of the angel. In the distance, she could hear the fading *clip clop* of camels' hooves.

After the Wise Men left their gifts of gold, frankincense, and myrrh. . .
After they mounted camels to return to the East. . .

Three wise women shared
God's great Gift with the whole world.

Mémère,
    You're one of my
wise women!
            Sue